Adapted by Jasmine Jones
Based on the series created by
Michael Poryes
Susan Sherman
Part One is based on the teleplay written by
Laura Perkins-Brittain & Carla Banks Waddles
Part Two is based on the teleplay written by
Beth Seriff & Geoff Tarson

New York

Printed in the United States of America

First Edition
1 3 5 7 9 10 8 6 4 2

Library of Congress Control Number: 2004112618

ISBN 0-7868-4660-7

For more Disney Press fun, visit www.disneybooks.com
Visit DisneyChannel.com

Part One

Chapter One

"**N**o, Tanya, there's no need to worry," Raven's father, Victor Baxter, said into the phone.

Sitting at the breakfast table, Raven could hear her mother's voice blaring from the receiver, even though her father was on the other side of the kitchen. Raven's mom was visiting her parents, which meant that her dad was in charge. Mrs. Baxter was usually cool as a cucumber, Raven noted, but she always went halfway to mental when she left home, as if she thought the family might fall apart while she was away, or something.

"Everything is running smoothly here," Mr. Baxter assured his wife. Just then, the toaster popped up. Raven's dad held out a plate and caught the toast as it sailed through the air. Now that *was* smooth, Raven thought.

"Rae, will you tell your mother everything's fine?" Mr. Baxter asked, handing her the cordless phone and setting the plate of toast down in front of her.

"Hi, Mom," Raven said into the phone. "We haven't eaten for days, your plants are dead, and I'm dropping out of school. Love ya. Bye." She absently brushed a piece of lint from her black sweater as she handed the phone back to her dad, who looked horrified. Oops, Raven thought. I forgot that Mom has zero sense of humor when it comes to being away from home.

"It was a *joke*," Mr. Baxter insisted into the receiver as he placed a sandwich stuffed with gourmet meats and cheeses in Cory's lunch box. Raven's dad was a chef, which meant Raven and Cory had the best lunches in the

Bay Area. Of course, it made the cafeteria food, when they had to eat it, seem a whole lot worse.

"No, no, Cory's a big boy," Mr. Baxter told his wife. "I let him pick out his clothes for school."

Just then, Cory walked into the kitchen wearing flip-flops, Hawaiian shorts, a tank top . . . and a giant inflatable duck-shaped inner tube around his waist.

Uh-uh, Raven thought. Now, I know that isn't *my* brother dressed like some kind of Orange Bowl float. Wherever Raven got her fashion sense from, the genes had definitely not been passed on to Cory. What he had was more like fashion *non*sense.

"Uh, Cory can't come to the phone right now," Mr. Baxter said quickly, eyeing Cory's outfit. "But I'll send him your love. Tell your folks I said hello. Bye-bye." Mr. Baxter hung up the phone and faced his son. "Cory, what do you have on?" he asked.

"I'm making a statement," Cory announced. "This says, 'Hi, I'm Cory. Wanna float my boat?'"

"Oh, really?" Raven said. "'Cause I'm hearing, 'Hi, I'm Cory. Wanna beat me up?'"

"Cory, go upstairs and put on something that doesn't quack," Mr. Baxter commanded, folding his arms across his chest.

Raven stood up and took her plate of untouched toast to the kitchen counter.

"Come on, Rae," her dad griped, "you've got to eat something before you go to school."

"I'm too nervous, Dad," Raven insisted. "They're announcing who's getting the parts in *The Wizard of Oz* today." Okay, so I haven't had a psychic vision about it, Raven thought, but I have a feeling that there will be a bunch of singing munchkins in my future.

"Let me guess," Mr. Baxter said, grabbing Raven's long black braids and giving them a gentle tug. "You're going up for the role of Dorothy."

"Yes, Dad, but I already made my costume. Say good-bye to Dorothy's frumpy blue little farm dress. And say hello to her new mini." Raven held up her latest fashion creation, a blue-and-white checked miniskirt trimmed in sparkly tulle.

Mr. Baxter frowned. "If Dorothy is still skipping down the yellow brick road, that hemline better come *way* down."

Raven looked at the skirt again. Okay, Dad does have a point, she had to admit.

"Come on, Cory!" Mr. Baxter hollered up the stairs. He turned to Raven. "I've got to get to the restaurant early today," he said. "The new owner, Mr. Briggs? Two words: not nice."

Cory appeared at the bottom of the stairs,

dressed more or less as a normal human being in jeans and a striped shirt. "I'm ready now," he said, glaring at his father. "My creativity has been squashed, but I am ready."

"Well, good luck with the new boss," Raven told her dad.

"Oh, come on, Rae, I get along with everybody." Mr. Baxter waved his hand dismissively and handed Cory his lunch box. "That restaurant has had lots of owners, but only one chef . . . your old man. Now, please, please . . ." He grabbed a bright green apple out of the fruit bowl and handed it to Raven. "Eat something," he told her. He kissed Raven on the forehead, then followed Cory out the back door.

"Okay, okay," Raven promised, taking the apple.

Suddenly, the world began to spin. The kitchen went hazy, and Raven felt as though time had frozen. . . .

Through her eye
The vision runs
Flash of future
Here it comes—

Where am I? It looks like Augustine's, the restaurant where Dad works.

Hey, look, there's Dad! He looks so much taller in his chef's hat. But who's that weaselly little guy with the sour face? He looks as pinched as a dried-up old apple.

"I've heard enough out of you, Baxter!" the man says. "You're fired!"

Oh, no. I just realized who that man is. It's Mr. Briggs, Dad's new boss.

And Dad is about to get terminated!

Raven came out of her vision and swallowed hard. That vision was no joke. She had to warn her dad!

Chapter Two

"**Y**ou guys, I just had a really bad vision," Raven said later at school. She was walking down the hall with her two best friends, Eddie Thomas and Chelsea Daniels. "I saw that my dad is going to get fired today."

Eddie looked at Raven, concerned. "Now, that's *deep*," he said.

"I know," Raven agreed. "I keep calling the restaurant, but the line's busy. I've got to go down there at lunch and warn him."

"Rae, since you're going down there, could you grab me one of your dad's desserts?" Eddie asked hopefully.

Raven stared at him. Sometimes, it was hard to believe just how one-track Eddie's mind could be. "Yeah, sure, Eddie," Raven said, her voice heavy with sarcasm. "While I'm down there, I'll just be, like, 'Hey, Dad, you're gonna get fired. Oh, but before you do, could you grab me a cheesecake?'" She rolled her eyes and whacked Eddie playfully on the shoulder.

"This is it, you guys," Chelsea said as the three friends stopped in front of a classroom door. "Drama Club. People go in with high hopes and come out with . . ." Chelsea's voice dropped to a trembling whisper. ". . . crushed dreams." She turned to Raven and smiled so brightly that her eyebrows disappeared beneath her straight, red bangs. "So, you ready?"

"I *was*," Raven said, giving Chelsea a look. She loved Chelsea, but sometimes the girl seemed to be broadcasting from a distant planet.

"Just remember," Eddie said, "if we don't get

the parts we want, it doesn't change who we are on the inside."

Five minutes later, Eddie was singing a different tune, and it went something like this: "I got the part! I'm the Scarecrow! My life has meaning!" He danced around the classroom, then turned to Señorita Rodriguez, the Drama Club's faculty advisor. "I must have had the best audition, huh?"

Señorita Rodriguez nodded, smiling. "No," she told him flatly.

The smile disappeared from Eddie's face.

"But Rodney is sick," Señorita Rodriguez explained.

Eddie shrugged and looked around at the rest of the drama clubbers. "I still got it," he said defensively. Then he went around the room, slapping high fives.

Note to self, Raven thought as she watched Eddie strut, remember to be *modest* when you get the part of Dorothy. In the interest of being generous, Raven turned to Kayla, her competition, who was sitting on the stool next to hers. "I just wanted to say," Raven told her, "no matter who gets the part, no hard feelings."

"Oh, how sweet," Kayla said, flashing Raven a big, phony smile. "I should say something nice to you." She tossed her long, dark pigtails over her shoulders and thought for a moment. Then she shrugged. "I got nothin'."

Raven leaned in the other direction, toward Chelsea. "Hate her," the two friends chorused under their breath.

"And now," Señorita Rodriguez said as she stood at the front of the classroom, clutching her clipboard, "after careful consideration, I have decided that the crucial role of Dorothy will be played by . . ." She looked at the chart in her hand and frowned. "Raven—"

Raven leaped off her stool and clenched her fists in victory. "Yes!" she hissed.

"I *thought* you were here." Señorita Rodriguez made a note on her clipboard, shaking her head. "Why did I mark you absent?"

Is there any way to make it look like I just hopped off my stool to stretch? Raven wondered as she skulked back to her seat. No? Okay, then. I'll just sit back down.

"Okay, where was I?" Señorita Rodriguez went on.

"Dorothy?" Raven whispered.

"Oh, yes, such a fun part," Señorita Rodriguez said. "And it will be played by Kayla Simms."

"I don't believe it!" Kayla squealed in her best hand-me-an-Oscar voice. "Is this real? Somebody pinch me!"

Raven leaned over and gave Kayla what she'd asked for.

"Ow!" Kayla shouted, glaring at Raven.

"Guess it's real," Raven hissed, smiling through clenched teeth.

"Rae, don't worry about it, okay?" Chelsea told her friend. "It's just a part, it's not a big deal."

Señorita Rodriguez cleared her throat. "And the Wicked Witch of the West will be . . . Chelsea Daniels."

"Yes!" Chelsea screeched, leaping up from her stool. "I got the part! That's right! Who's your witch?" She turned to the drama clubbers and framed her face with her hands, vogue style. "Who's your witch? Who's your witch?" Chelsea turned to Raven and demanded, "Who's your witch?"

Raven shot her a deadly glare.

"Not that it's any big deal," Chelsea added quickly, sitting back down again.

Yeah, right, Raven thought. It's not a big deal to anyone—but me.

Chapter Three

"**V**ictor, what is this?"

At the sound of the nasal voice, Raven's dad turned to see his boss, Mr. Briggs, standing next to him. He was holding one of Mr. Baxter's special appetizers. Mr. Baxter smiled proudly. "It's my famous stuffed artichoke," he replied.

"No," Mr. Briggs corrected, "it's your famous *huge* artichoke. Huge means I pay more for it." His pinched face turned absolutely prunelike as it wrinkled in disgust. "I *hate* huge."

"Mr. Briggs, I personally handpicked this produce myself," Mr. Baxter explained. Every morning, Raven's dad stopped by the farmers' market to get the freshest, most delicious ingredients. "My motto is, 'The customers always come back when quality is the main ingredient.'"

Mr. Briggs looked as though Mr. Baxter had just fed him a lemon. "Really?" he asked. "My motto is, 'I own the place.'" He shoved the artichoke plate into Mr. Baxter's hands. "Go salt something," he commanded with a dismissive wave, then strutted off toward the maître d' stand.

Mr. Baxter raised the artichoke as though he might hurl it at his whiny little boss. Mercifully, at that moment a waiter walked out of the kitchen and grabbed the plate from Mr. Baxter's hand. "Thank you!" he said brightly, heading over to a table with the appetizer.

Just then, Raven walked into the restaurant and looked around. Everything seemed normal. Her father was at his usual place behind the counter in front of the kitchen.

He's still chopping something and he's still wearing his tall white chef's hat, Raven thought, so nothing has happened yet. I just need to talk to Mr. Briggs and convince him not to fire my dad. And there he is, Raven realized, recognizing the sour-looking man from her vision.

"Hi," Raven said brightly, walking up to him. "I'm Raven. Mr. Baxter's daughter."

Mr. Briggs gave her a tense smile. "Hello, how are you, nice to—buh-bye." He looked back down at his reservations book.

Dang, Raven thought, forget "not nice." Her dad was too kind. Mr. Briggs was a nasty little restaurant troll! She would have walked out right then and there, but she'd had a vision. And she was going to do everything in her power to keep it from coming true.

"Uh, I don't mean to bother you—" she began.

"—and yet, here you stand," Mr. Briggs finished for her.

Be nice, Raven commanded herself silently. She smiled and started again. "I just wanted to say that, you know, my dad is really passionate about food." Mr. Briggs's icy glare almost made her stop, but she forced herself to go on. "And that's what makes him a great chef. I mean, you are totally lucky to have him. Tons of great restaurants are dying to have him."

Mr. Briggs blinked. "Really? Is that so?" He walked off, greeting customers as he passed their tables with a tense whisper of "Hi, how are you?"

Ugh, is he trying to make them lose their appetites? Raven wondered. Because that grimace on his face is about to make me lose mine. Still, she had come here to do a job, and she wasn't going to get sidetracked that easily.

"Yes," Raven said quickly, following him.

"Yes. Very so. Since you have him, hold on to him really tight." She held up her hands, balling her fingers into fists for emphasis.

That seemed to get Mr. Briggs's attention. He stopped in his tracks. "I'll tell you, since you're following me anyway . . ."

Raven giggled nervously, and Mr. Briggs laughed along.

"I think your father is a wonderful chef," the restaurant owner explained. "And I'm very happy with him. Okay?"

"Okay, that is what I wanted to hear," Raven replied, heaving a sigh of relief. Now that was *way* easier than I thought it would be, she thought. That's right—psychic in the house, savin' the day.

"Oh, good," Mr. Briggs said brightly. "You know what I wanted to hear?"

Raven thought for a moment. "Buh-bye?" she guessed.

"Oh, you're good." Mr. Briggs turned and gave his customers a huge fake smile.

You're not the only one who's glad this conversation is over, Raven thought as she turned to leave. But just as Raven reached the door, she came face-to-face with her dad, who had rushed away from his station the minute he saw her talking to Mr. Briggs.

"What are you doing here?" Mr. Baxter asked worriedly.

"What am I doing here?" Raven repeated, stalling for time. Think of something good, she told herself. You can't tell Dad that you came down here to save his job.

Luckily, Raven's dad did her thinking for her. "Let me guess," he said, his worried expression turning to a grin, "you got the part of Dorothy."

Raven took a deep breath. "No," she said. "I didn't get it."

Mr. Baxter's face fell. "I'm so sorry, baby."

"That's okay," Raven said quickly. And it really was okay . . . well, kind of. The truth was that she had momentarily forgotten all about the part—saving her dad's job was much more important. "That's what I came here for," she improvised. "To tell you that, and that I'm okay with it."

Mr. Baxter grinned proudly. "That's the Rae I know."

"So," Raven said, wrapping her dad in a warm hug, "I'm going back to school and you, Daddy, have a great day." Smiling, she waved and took off.

Mr. Baxter watched her go. Then he caught sight of Mr. Briggs. "So, I see you met my daughter, Raven," he said to his boss. "She's really a great kid."

"Really?" Mr. Briggs said doubtfully. "She must be having an off day."

Mr. Baxter stared at him, then shook his head. He was starting to think that maybe he had been wrong about his new boss. It seemed like "not nice" was the understatement of the century.

Chapter Four

"**O**kay," Raven said to Chelsea and Eddie later that day. They were standing in Raven's living room, getting ready to work on their lines for the play. "Before we start rehearsal, I just would like to say, there's so much stuff I could do with this part." She gestured to the script in her hand.

"That's cool, Rae," Chelsea said. "But really, uh, you're the Wicked Witch of the East. Your part is lying under a house."

"Yeah," Eddie agreed. "Get under the coffee table and stick your feet out."

"No, no, no, no." Raven shook her head. Her friends clearly weren't tuning into Raven's vision of the role. The Wicked Witch of the

East is a part that's waiting to happen, Raven thought. I just have to work with it. "You don't get it," Raven said. "See, I've been working on this part. I call this, 'Death of a Witch.'"

Raven passed a hand over her face, getting into character. She cleared her throat, then started to sing the original song she had written that afternoon on the school bus. Raven liked to think of it as the *Wizard of Oz's* "lost scene."

"*Something's coming . . .*" Raven belted out in an operatic voice. She pretended to gaze into the distance. "*It's a house . . .*" Raven leaped up onto the coffee table. "*I'll be under it . . . in this blouse . . .*" She yanked at her shirt theatrically. "*I just bought today.*" Hmm, maybe I should write the scene where the Wicked Witch of the East goes clothes shopping, Raven thought, launching into the elaborate choreography she'd prepared. After all, even witches have to look good, she added silently as she busted her moves all over the coffee table.

"Rae! Rae!" Eddie shouted, hauling Raven off the coffee table. "Let me show you," he said slowly. "You're a squished witch, all right? Okay, lay down right here." He helped Raven onto the floor beneath the coffee table. Once she was lying there with her legs sticking out, he crowed, "*That's* what you do."

Raven heaved a frustrated sigh and sat up. "You know what?" she said, hauling herself to her feet. "This is a lame part. I'm going to tell Señorita Rodriguez I quit."

Just then, Raven heard keys jingle in the lock, and the front door swung open.

"Hey, Mr. Baxter," Eddie said as Raven's father walked into the living room.

"Hi, Mr. Baxter," Chelsea chimed in.

"Dad!" Raven said in surprise. "What are you doing home so early?"

"What kind of greeting is that?" Mr. Baxter demanded. "How about, 'Dad's home! Let's par-tay!'" Raven's dad did a little dance move, gave them a double thumbs-up, then headed for the kitchen.

Chelsea smiled after him. "He's sure in a good mood," she said.

Raven frowned. "No. Something's wrong," she said. Her stomach gave a nervous flutter as she followed her father into the kitchen, where Mr. Baxter was busy shaking salt into a pot.

"Dad," Raven asked gently, "are you okay?"

"Yeah," Mr. Baxter replied. "I'm fine. Just making a little soup."

Raven reached into the pot. "It might be a little less chunky without the can," she suggested, holding it up.

Mr. Baxter stared at the can of soup as

though he had no idea where it had come from. Not a good sign, Raven thought.

"What's going on?" she asked, afraid to hear the answer.

"Oh, nothing," Mr. Baxter said carefully. "I just got into a little argument with Mr. Briggs." He wiped salt off the can and set it down on the table.

"Dad, what happened?" Raven asked. "When I left, everything seemed . . . great."

"You know, nothing's ever great with that guy," Mr. Baxter griped. "He even had a problem with you coming down today. Like you even said more than two words to him."

A problem . . . with me? Raven thought. Her stomach sank. Oh, no. I mean, I didn't really bother him . . . that much. How many words *did* I say to him? "Two," she admitted. "Maybe three. Four, Dad, tops."

"And he said if I have a problem with

the way he wants things done, then I could go work for one of the 'tons of restaurants that were dying to hire me.'" Raven's dad looked as though that was the craziest thing he had ever heard. "I don't know where he got that from."

Raven winced, wishing that she could say the same thing—only she *did* know where Mr. Briggs got that from, because she had given it to him. "You got fired, didn't you?" she asked quietly. Please say no, Raven begged silently. Please say—

"Yeah, baby," Mr. Baxter admitted. "I got fired." He pointed to Raven reassuringly. "But everything's going to be okay."

Raven had to swallow hard to clear the lump in her throat. If I hadn't gone down to Augustine's and tried to convince Mr. Briggs not to fire Dad, she thought, he never would have thought of letting him go.

"Dad, I'm so sorry," she told her father.

"Baby, don't be." Mr. Baxter held her by the shoulders and looked her in the eye. "It's not like it's your fault." Then he wrapped his arms around Raven and gave her a hug.

But Raven couldn't get past the guilt she was feeling. After all, it *was* her fault. She was sure of it.

Chapter Five

"**R**ae, it is not your fault your dad got fired," Chelsea said that night.

The two girls were sitting on Raven's bed. Chelsea had stayed for dinner with the Baxters, and the minute she put down her fork, Raven had called an emergency meeting in her room. She needed to talk this out. She was so upset she could hardly think straight.

"But if I didn't go down there and bother his boss, my dad would still have a job," Raven protested.

"That is so true," Cory said, bursting into Raven's room. "Stand here. Hold this." He handed Raven the end of a measuring tape, then walked to the far window. "Nine feet," he announced, checking the measurement. "Yup. My bed can go right here." Cory gave Raven a smug smile.

"Excuse me," Raven snapped, "what are you doing?"

"Making sure all my stuff is going to fit," Cory replied. "'Cause when Dad finds out you got him fired, you'll be history. And this," he said, gesturing at Raven's room, "will all be mine." Looking up at Chelsea, he waggled his eyebrows. "Hey, baby, like my new crib?" he asked smoothly.

Raven let go of the measuring tape, and it snapped back into the case in Cory's hand.

Chelsea ignored Cory and turned back to her friend. "Rae, just go talk to Mr. Briggs," she said. "Tell him you're sorry, and maybe he'll hire your dad back."

Cory looked around the room and pointed to Raven's purple window trim. "This paint has got to go," he said.

Raven narrowed her eyes at him. "Look, munchkin, I've had enough of you," she said, grabbing Cory by the collar and yanking him toward the door. "I'm going to the restaurant tomorrow to get Dad's job back, and until then . . . hey, you see the finger?" She wagged her index finger, and Cory followed it with his eyes. "You see the finger? You see the finger? The finger is looking at the room, and the finger says . . . the room is mine." Raven pointed at herself and glared at her brother.

The finger gave a little wave good-bye as Cory scurried out the door.

"Hi," Raven said brightly as she walked up to Mr. Briggs the next afternoon. "Me again."

Mr. Briggs barely glanced up from the

reservation book. "Oh, goody," he said sarcastically. "Wishes do come true."

"Yes," Raven replied, smiling bravely, "and *I* wish that you'd hire my dad back."

Mr. Briggs looked at Raven. "And then, some wishes don't." He walked off to grimace at the customers in his tense little way.

Don't take no for an answer, Raven told herself firmly. "I don't think my dad should be fired because of my mistake," she said, following Mr. Briggs.

"You know," Mr. Briggs said, "I think it's *nifty* that you came all the way down here to stick up for your dad. Right a wrong." Mr. Briggs paused, his pinched face screwed up in thought. "Ever notice how nifty people never win?" He shook his head. "Your dad's not getting his job back."

Raven decided to try another tactic. "Hey, Mr. Briggs, you don't fool me, okay? You try to talk tough, but I can see that you're very kind, sensitive, warm, forgiving." This was a complete lie, but hey—Raven was willing to try anything.

"Dear child, you see right through me," Mr. Briggs said. "Listen, Robin—"

"Raven," she corrected.

"Whatever," Mr. Briggs said. "A little advice, kid. Kissing up will get you nowhere."

Just then, the door to Augustine's flew open, and a group of people decked out in expensive hip-hop rags strode in. Beaming, Mr. Briggs rushed over to greet the cool, leather-clad man in the center of the pack.

"Hellooo, Mr. Q-Z!" Mr. Briggs said brightly. "So nice to see you again. Q-Z in the hizhouse." He tried to knock fists with the star, but it looked more like he was trying to play patty-cake with a professional boxer. "Peace to the brothers," Mr. Briggs finished weakly.

Wow, Raven thought as she watched Mr. Briggs desperately try to be "down." I see what he means. Kissing up really *doesn't* get you anywhere.

"I see you brought the whole . . ." Mr. Briggs racked his brain for the right lingo. "Posse," he said finally. "I have your table for you. Love your last video—it was . . . slammin'."

Raven watched as Mr. Briggs led Q-Z and his peeps to the best table in the house. Suddenly, her face lit up in a smile.

Raven had an idea. And it was *diva-licious.*

Chapter Six

"**A**ll right! Everybody step back!" Eddie announced as he strode through the doors of Augustine's. He was wearing an enormous Afro wig and a leather jacket, and his neck was weighted down with heavy gold chains.

Chelsea was right behind him, wearing sunglasses and a short red wig. "Famous person coming through," she called out in a phony English accent.

And that was when Raven made her entrance.

Only it wasn't Raven Baxter who walked into Augustine's. It was a glamorous diva in oversized shades and a glittery jumpsuit that looked like it had recently escaped from Las

Vegas. To top off her disguise, Raven had on a long, platinum blond wig tipped in neon pink.

Raven looked like a hip-hop star, complete with her own entourage. And we expect some service, Raven thought as everyone in the room turned to stare.

Mr. Briggs's eyes widened as he hurried over to Raven and her friends. "Welcome to Augustine's," he said.

"Two steps back," Eddie barked and Mr. Briggs hopped to obey.

"Please stop looking at me!" Raven begged at the top of her lungs in an accent that was half Jamaican, half British—and *all* diva. "Why can't I just blend in?" She gave her long blond hair a dramatic toss with her two-inch-long, wine-colored fingernails.

An excited murmur rippled through the restaurant.

"We'd like our usual table," Raven told Mr. Briggs.

Mr. Briggs looked blank. "Your usual table?"

"He's looking me in the eye!" Raven wailed.

Eddie scowled at Mr. Briggs. "Don't do that," he told him.

Mr. Briggs averted his eyes.

"Do you know who I be?" Raven demanded, tapping Mr. Briggs on the head. "Do you listen to music?"

"Do you watch TV?" Eddie put in.

"Do you carry a lunch box?" Chelsea added, her exaggerated English accent giving her question even more authority.

"Eddie," Raven snapped, "tell him who I be."

Eddie stared at Raven through his dark shades. "Me?"

"You don't expect *me* to introduce *me*, do

you?" Raven asked, gesturing to her sparkly jumpsuit. Oh, come on, Eddie, Raven thought. Play along. No superstar in a sequined getup can introduce herself. It just isn't done.

"Well, uh . . ." Eddie hedged, glancing around the restaurant in desperation. "That's, uh . . ." At that moment, a waiter walked by carrying two steaming plates of delicious-smelling food. Eddie's eyes followed the plates hungrily, and a single word dropped from his lips: "Lasagna."

I know I didn't hear that right, Raven thought.

"Liz Anya," Eddie corrected, realizing what he had said.

Luckily, Mr. Briggs didn't seem to be too up on the current music scene. "Oh!" he said, as though he was a huge Liz Anya fan. "Right, right, right, right. Right this way, Ms. Anya."

Gesturing for the entourage to follow him, Mr. Briggs led them toward the best table in the house.

While his back was turned, Raven leaned toward Eddie. "Liz Anya?" she growled.

"Hey," Eddie snapped back, "you were almost Pork Choppa."

I guess I should be grateful that I'm not named after a piece of grilled pig, Raven thought as she sat down at the table. She waved away the menu that Mr. Briggs was holding out to her. "I don't need a menu. Just have Victor prepare my usual," she said. She took a sip of her water.

Mr. Briggs looked crestfallen, and Raven had to hide a tiny smile in her water glass. Serves you right for firing my dad, she thought.

"Victor doesn't work here anymore," Mr. Briggs admitted finally.

Raven, Eddie, and Chelsea simultaneously spit out the water they had just sipped.

"Are you joking?" Raven shouted, pounding the table theatrically.

Mr. Briggs winced. "Shhh . . ."

"Don't shush her," Eddie warned.

"This restaurant is nothing without Victor!" Raven cried in her unidentifiable accent. She was really getting into her role. "Where is he?"

"You know," Chelsea trilled to Mr. Briggs, "if I were you, I'd get Victor back now before she—"

"Get me J.Lo!" Raven barked.

"Oh!" Chelsea said dramatically, gasping as though she had been slammed in the gut. "It's too late!"

Chelsea pulled a cell phone from her pocket and punched in a number. She handed Raven the phone as Mr. Briggs stood by, watching the scene in horror. "Hey, girlfriend,"

Raven said into the phone. "Yeah, let me tell you something. I'm down here at Augustine's, and this fool . . ." She glared at Mr. Briggs. ". . . fired our Victor. I know. No, she—all right." Raven held out the phone to Mr. Briggs. "She wants to speak to you."

Mr. Briggs looked at the phone as though he thought it might reach out and slap him. "Jennifer Lopez wants to speak to me?"

"Don't look at the phone, brother," Eddie warned him.

Tentatively, Mr. Briggs took the phone from Chelsea. "Hello . . . Ms. Lopez? I just want to say I'm a big, big fan—"

"Don't you sweet-talk me!" the voice on the other end shouted.

Raven smiled as a high-pitched voice poured from the phone. Of course, Mr. Briggs didn't need to know that the J.Lo he had on the phone was actually Cory, who had agreed to help Raven get their dad's job back . . . for ten dollars and a bag of Doritos.

"Not after what you did to my Victor!" Cory screeched into the phone. "You wanna see my back? Then get Victor back." Slamming down the phone, Cory looked up just in time to see his father standing behind him, wide-eyed.

For a minute, Cory just stood there, unsure what to do. "Mom says all boys' voices change at this age," Cory finally improvised in a high-pitched squeal. "And anyone who makes fun of me is just *mean*." He stalked out of the kitchen in a huff as Mr. Baxter stared after him, speechless.

Meanwhile, back at the restaurant, Raven was taking things to a whole new level.

"The only reason I came here is for Victor's cooking," she shouted. "And I'm sure I'm not the only one. 'Scuse me." Raven yanked a plate away from a woman at a nearby table. "Victor never would've served an artichoke that scrawny!" she declared. Yanking a long blond hair from her wig, Raven pretended to pull it out of a woman's plate. "Victor never would have used *this* ingredient in his cooking," she said, indicating the hair. The woman looked horrified. "Send that back," Raven suggested. She started to storm out of the restaurant, followed by Chelsea and Eddie, but a waiter stopped them.

"Excuse me," the waiter said, "some customers are wondering if you'll sing something off your new CD." He smiled hopefully at Raven.

Raven stopped in her tracks. "They are?" she asked. Wow, she said to herself. I guess my diva act is even more convincing than I thought!

"Oh, that's a wonderful idea—please sing!" Mr. Briggs begged, shoving the waiter out of the way. "It will be wonderful for business. Sing something, please."

The customers began to applaud in anticipation.

Wonderful for business, eh? Raven thought. An idea was slowly forming in her mind. "No, I'm not sure," she told Mr. Briggs.

"No, no, no!" Chelsea scoffed. "She cannot just sing cold. I mean, *really*."

"Liz Anya's always better warmed up, brother," Eddie agreed.

"I'll consider hiring Victor back," Mr. Briggs volunteered.

That was all Raven needed to hear. "It's showtime!" she shouted, flinging her hands in the air.

The customers cheered as Raven led Eddie and Chelsea toward the baby grand piano in the corner. "I think I'll do a song I just wrote," she said, grabbing a microphone from the top of the piano.

Eddie stared down at the keyboard. "I only know one song," he whispered to Raven. And I haven't had a lesson since I was eight years old, he added silently.

"Then just play it," Raven hissed. "And make it funky." Smiling, she said into the microphone, "And it goes a little something like this."

Eddie plunked a few keys.

Dang, Raven thought, as Eddie fumbled across the keys. That sounds like "When the Saints Go Marching In" . . . if it was being played by a cat with a can tied to its tail. I'll just have to improvise, she told herself. She tried to give the old song a little funk with a few dance moves.

"*Oh, when the saints,*" Raven sang, "*go*

marching in. Oh, when the saints go marching in. Oh my, I want to be in that number, when the saints go marching in." The customers started to clap as Raven got into the song. "Take it, papi!" she shouted.

"*Oh, when the saints,*" Chelsea and Eddie sang, taking over the chorus as Raven strutted around the restaurant.

"That steak is rare!" Raven shouted in time to the music, pointing at the meat on a woman's plate.

"*Go marching in . . .*"

"I think it mooed!" Raven sang. She handed the plate to Mr. Briggs.

"*Oh, when the saints go marching in . . .*"

"Oooh," Raven said, sniffing one customer's plate. "Too much garlic." She handed the plate to Mr. Briggs, saying, "Take this."

"*I want to be in that number!*"

"She ain't kissin' you good night," Raven

told the over-garlicked customer, then rejoined the song. "*When the saints go marching in.*"

Raven decided it was time to make the song a little more to the point. "*Since Victor left,*" she sang, "*the food's no good. Since Victor left, the food's no good. It's undercooked and poorly seasoned. Since Victor left, the food's no good.*"

A few women stood up and joined in the song. "*Since Victor left, the food's no good,*" they sang, belting out the words like a gospel choir. Raven marched around the restaurant in time to the music, and the other women followed, singing their hearts out. "*Since Victor left, the food's no good. It's undercooked and poorly seasoned. Since Victor left, the food's no good.*" The whole restaurant joined in, clapping and singing. It was off the hook!

Chelsea watched as her friend led the restaurant in a musical revolt. Raven is truly amazing, she thought. And those drama lessons really paid off!

Just then, Señorita Rodriguez and her husband walked into the restaurant.

"*Tell Mr. Briggs,*" Raven sang, giving her powerful pipes a workout.

Chelsea nudged Eddie, whose eyes went wide at the sight of their drama teacher. "*Look over there!*" he and Chelsea sang.

But Raven wasn't listening. She was busy leading her choir in a rousing chorus of "*get Victor back!*"

Eddie and Chelsea tried again. "*Right over there!*"

"*Tell Mr. Briggs, get Victor back,*" Raven belted out.

Finally, Chelsea and Eddie had to stop being subtle—it was obviously lost on Raven. "*It's Rodriguez!*" Chelsea and Eddie sang.

Raven looked shocked, but she didn't lose a

beat. "*I'd better wrap up this number,*" she sang. "*Tell Mr. Briggs, get Victor back.*"

The audience applauded.

"I'll bring him back!" Mr. Briggs cried, joining the song.

That's the line I've been waiting for! Raven thought. "I love you all!" she cried, blowing kisses to the crowd. "And, more importantly, you love me!" She looked toward the door, but it was still blocked by their drama teacher.

"Through the kitchen!" Raven whispered to Eddie and Chelsea, and the three friends scurried behind Victor's counter. But just as they headed for the kitchen door, it swung open. They collided with a waiter who was struggling beneath a heavy tray.

Crash! Raven, her friends, and the waiter all went down.

Raven's wig fell off, and she scrambled to stick it back on her head before anyone noticed. Eddie and Chelsea were also trying to pull themselves together in the mess.

At last, the three friends peeped over the counter, hoping that no one had noticed their fall.

But as she stood up, Raven saw Mr. Briggs glaring at her. She tried to walk away coolly, but the restaurant owner blocked her path.

"I know," Raven said. "You recognize greatness."

Mr. Briggs shook his head. "No, Antipasti."

"Lasagna," Raven corrected.

"Whatever," Mr. Briggs snapped. "I recognize *you*." His face twisted into a grin as he yanked the wig off her head. "Don't you just hate it when the bad guy wins?" Narrowing his eyes at Eddie, he added, "Don't look at me."

"Oh, of course not," Eddie said quickly, hiding his face behind the long blond strands of his wig.

Long blond strands? Looking up, Raven realized that in the confusion, their wigs had gotten switched. Now Eddie was wearing the long blond wig, Raven was wearing Chelsea's short red wig, and Chelsea had on Eddie's giant Afro.

It turned out that Mr. Briggs wasn't the only one who had recognized Raven. As Raven and her friends trudged toward the exit, Señorita Rodriguez stopped her before she could walk out the door. "Raven!" she said, with an enormous smile. "I was wrong. You have a lovely voice. You should have played Dorothy."

A slow, hopeful smile spread across Raven's face. "So I get the part?" she asked eagerly.

Señorita Rodriguez nodded her head. "No," she said.

Raven sighed. Her father didn't have his job back, and she *still* didn't get to play Dorothy, even though she'd just given the performance of a lifetime.

Looks like this Liz Anya got burned, Raven thought.

Chapter Seven

"**U**h-huh," Mr. Baxter said into the phone later that evening.

Raven sat at the kitchen table, fidgeting nervously. She'd barely had time to change her clothes and rinse the spaghetti sauce out of her hair before Mr. Briggs called. He had been screeching into Mr. Baxter's ear for half an hour, and Raven really didn't want to hear what her punishment was going to be. I'm looking at a life sentence, Raven thought glumly. Isn't that the minimum for getting your father fired?

"Yeah, but Mr. Briggs . . ." Mr. Baxter went on. "She said *that*? But . . . but—" The dial tone buzzed from the phone; Mr. Briggs had finally hung up. "Oh, whatever," Mr. Baxter said, clicking the off button and putting down the phone. "That was Mr. Briggs, Raven," he said, eyeing his daughter. "Or should I say, *Lasagna*?"

Raven sighed. Please don't tell me I'm going to be stuck with that stupid nickname for the rest of my life, she thought. Things are bad enough already.

"I don't think I've ever heard him that mad before," Mr. Baxter said. Suddenly, the scowl on his face disappeared, replaced with a grin. "Way to go, Raven."

Raven's mouth fell open in shock. "So, Dad, you're okay?"

"Absolutely." Mr. Baxter picked up a knife and sliced into the vanilla cake with chocolate frosting he'd baked that day. "You know, sometimes bad news is really opportunity in disguise," he told Raven. "Like when I was in high school on the football team. It was home-coming weekend, and I got hurt really bad—"

Raven winced sympathetically. "Oh, Dad, what happened? A bad tackle?"

"No, they cut me from the team." Mr. Baxter sighed. "That hurt really bad."

Raven rolled her eyes. "Thanks for the tip, Dad."

"No," Mr. Baxter said as he set the piece of cake on the table and sat down beside Raven. "My point is, because I didn't have to go to practice, I had more free time. So I started hanging out with your grandma and helping her in the kitchen. And that's when I realized I loved to cook." He handed Raven a fork.

"You never told me that story," Raven said.

"Yeah, but see, the point of this story is, life is gonna knock you down sometimes, and that's okay. But what's not okay is when you let it keep you down." Mr. Baxter smiled at his daughter. "So everything's going to be okay. I'm not gonna be down for long."

Raven nodded, glancing up at the neon sign that decorated the wall of the Baxters' kitchen. BAXTER'S PLACE, it read.

Suddenly, her skin prickled, and her vision became hazy. She felt as though she was in another place, even though she hadn't moved. . . .

**Through her eye
The vision runs
Flash of future
Here it comes—**

Hey, where am I? This is the ritziest neighborhood in town.

Check out that stylin' new restaurant with the fancy awning. Looks like a nice place. But, hold on . . . there's something familiar

about the sign over the door. It says . . .
Baxter's Place.

Yeah, that has a nice ring to it.

That's it! Raven thought as she snapped out of
her vision. Dad is going to open his own
restaurant. Raven smiled at her father as she
dug into the slice of cake.

"I'm sure you'll think of something," she
told him.

"You know, Señorita Rodriguez," Raven told
her drama teacher the next day at school,
"even though I only got the part of the Wicked
Witch of the East, I'm okay with it. 'Cause I
figured, that's life. And I'm not going to let it
keep me down."

Señorita Rodriguez nodded approvingly.
"That's a good way to look at it, Raven," she
said.

"So," Raven went on, "since I don't have any lines, I'll have lots of free time. And I wanted to design the costumes for the show. So . . . introducing 'Scarecrow from the 'Hood.'"

Hearing his cue, Eddie slid into the drama room wearing a red-and-yellow, hip-hop-inspired scarecrow outfit.

"Come on, the 'Happenin' Wicked Witch!'" Raven called, and Chelsea walked in wearing a hot little purple-and-black dress embroidered with silver spiderwebs. "We ain't in Kansas no more," Raven said.

"Raven, these are wonderful," Señorita Rodriguez said. "You've got the job."

"Thank you!" Raven said, smiling. "Oops, forgot one. Yo, Munchkin," she hollered. "Get in here!"

Cory trudged in, looking absolutely miserable in a pair of bright purple knickers, a satin waistcoat, and a floppy hat. He was holding a giant cardboard lollipop. "Whose room is it again?" Raven asked him.

Cory scowled. "Your room," he muttered.

Raven pinched his cheek. "Good little munchkin," she said.

See? Raven thought as she grinned at her drama teacher. This job is made for me! Like Dad said, losing out on the role was just an opportunity in disguise.

"This says, 'Hi, I'm Cory. Wanna float my boat?'" he said.

"Say good-bye to Dorothy's frumpy little blue farm dress," Raven said.

"I call this, 'Death of a Witch,'" Raven said.

"Hey, you were almost Pork Choppa," Eddie said.

"Oh, when the saints go marching in,"
Raven sang.

The three friends peeped over the counter,
hoping that no one had noticed their fall.

"Life is going to knock you down sometimes, and that's okay. But what's not okay is when you let it keep you down," Mr. Baxter said.

"Good little munchkin," said Raven.

"Eddie, your head's on backwards," Raven said.

"Ooh, I like 'em fiesty," Cory said.

"Boy likes girl. Girl likes boy. They both die. Cry, cry, cry. The end," Raven said.

"I'm going to be your teacher for the rest of the year," Mrs. Baxter announced.

"Wow," Chelsea said when she saw the note.

"Mrs. Baxter, may I just say how much I enjoyed doing that homework assignment?" Eddie said.

"We're going in," said Raven.

"She was just singing that cool new song,"
Chelsea said quickly.

Part Two

Chapter One

As Raven and Chelsea walked into English class one morning, they met up with their friends Hallie and Jess, who were already standing at the front of the room. The four girls did their secret handshake—a complicated series of fist knocks and handclasps.

"Bam!" they shouted as they finished their moves, then they busted into giggles.

"Keepin' it live," Raven said, snapping her gum.

Just then, a supercute guy in a blue jacket walked past Raven. He had hazel eyes and light brown hair. Raven flashed him her pearly whites. "Heyyyyy, Eric," she said.

Eric smiled. "Hey."

Raven watched as Eric walked away. "He is so . . . *fine*," she said to Chelsea.

"Yeah. Mmm-mmm," Chelsea agreed enthusiastically. A bit *too* enthusiastically for Raven, who glared at her. "You know, for you," Chelsea added quickly, catching Raven's look. "All for you."

As the two friends headed toward their desks, Raven noticed that Eddie was already in his seat in the front row. But there was something very wrong with Eddie's outfit. He was wearing a red hooded sweatshirt . . . with the hood up over his face.

"Eddie," Raven said as she flipped down his hood, "your head's on backward."

"All part of the plan. Chill out," Eddie told her. He flipped the hood back up over his face.

"Pipe down, people!" Mr. Lawler, their English teacher, shouted from the front of the classroom. Spit flew everywhere, like a lawn sprinkler gone wild. "People, please!"

Mr. Lawler was a great teacher, but he had a peculiar spit problem. He also had an enormous vocabulary that seemed to include a lot of words that started with "p." Which meant, *nobody* wanted to sit in the front row of his class. But somehow Eddie had gotten stuck there.

But today Eddie thought he'd finally outsmarted spit-slingin' Lawler. He peeled off the hood and turned around in his seat, smiling smugly at Raven. "Whose head is on backward now?" he asked.

"First, an important announcement," Mr. Lawler sprayed.

Eddie winced as a shower of saliva rained down on him. I guess I spoke too soon, he thought miserably.

"I'm being promoted to principal," Mr.

Lawler went on. "Mr. Perkins was pushed up to superintendent."

It took a moment for the meaning of this pronouncement to dawn on Eddie. "You mean," he said slowly, "you won't be teaching right here anymore?" He pointed to the space directly in front of his desk.

Mr. Lawler let the spittle fly. "Precisely."

"I need a minute alone," Eddie said. Ducking out of his seat, Eddie headed for the classroom door.

What's Eddie all broken up about? Raven wondered, as she and Chelsea exchanged confused looks. A moment later, Raven understood. Through the window in the door, she caught a glimpse of Eddie doing a victory dance out in the hallway.

I guess Eddie pulled through after all, Raven decided.

Eddie walked back into the classroom and

gave a dramatic sniff. "I'll be okay," he told Mr. Lawler as he took his seat.

A kid named Max spoke up. "So now when you send me to the principal's office," he said to the teacher, "you'll be sending me . . . to *you*. Whoa!" He clutched his head. "Brain cramp!"

Raven rolled her eyes. Max was not the sharpest knife in the drawer. Actually, she thought, he's more like a rubber spatula.

"You'll have a substitute the rest of the week," Mr. Lawler explained. "And on Monday, there will be a new teacher."

Raven turned to Chelsea. "So who do you think the teacher's going to be?" she asked. "I hope it's not that whiny guy. You know, 'Please, students, all I ask is for y'all to sit down. *Please.*'" Raven screwed up her face, imitating the substitute begging for mercy.

Eddie and Chelsea cracked up. It *had* been fun messing with that guy.

"At least he's better than that paranoid lady," Chelsea said. "'Why are you talking about me?'" she cried in mock terror, mimicking the sub. "'I know you all hate me. I know you hate me, I know it.'"

"Ladies, talking," Mr. Lawler warned them. "Tragically, neither is available. We're having a heck of a time finding a substitute."

Just then, Raven's skin began to prickle and the world around her froze. . . .

Through her eye
The vision runs
Flash of future
Here it comes—

I'm right here in English class. I see a woman walking through the classroom door. Wait, I know that woman. It's . . . Mom? What's Mom doing at my school? Is she lost, or something? And why is she dressed up?

That's weird. She's walking up to Mr. Lawler's desk like she owns the place. And why is she carrying that stack of books?

"Hello, class," she says. "I'm your substitute, Mrs. Baxter."

Nooooooo!

Raven gasped and shook herself as she came out of the vision. "You're not going to believe this," she whispered, leaning toward her friends. "My mom is going to be the sub."

"Your mom?" Chelsea grinned. She thought Mrs. Baxter was way cool.

Raven nodded. "I know. I mean, she used to teach. But Mr. Lawler doesn't know that. He hasn't even met her before—"

"Raven!" a voice suddenly whispered.

Looking up, Raven saw her mom standing

in the doorway, holding a paper bag. "You forgot your lunch," Mrs. Baxter whispered.

"And he's not going to now," Raven growled, finishing her thought. She sprang out of her chair and hurried to the door. "Thanks, Mom," Raven said quickly, snatching the bag from her mother's hand. "That's sweet. Buh-bye."

"Mrs. Baxter," Mr. Lawler said as he walked up to Raven's mother and held out his hand. "I don't believe we've had the pleasure of meeting."

Mrs. Baxter winced as she got a mini shower, but she politely shook Mr. Lawler's hand.

"And now you have," Raven said quickly, gently nudging her mother toward the door. "So, once again, buh-bye. I've got learning to do."

Mrs. Baxter smiled at Mr. Lawler. "You

know, I wish my students were this eager back when I was teaching English."

"Mom!" And there it is, Raven thought. Cat, say good-bye to bag. She nervously snapped her gum.

"Well, I should go," Mrs. Baxter said, turning toward the door.

"You were an English teacher previously?" Mr. Lawler asked. This time, it was Raven who got sprayed in the face.

"Mrs. Baxter," Mr. Lawler said as he followed her into the hallway, "I just had the craziest idea!"

Raven watched with horror as Mr. Lawler continued talking to her mother. It was too late. There was no way to stop it.

Why couldn't it have been a vision about me and Eric? Raven wondered as she pressed her face against the window. *Why, why, why?*

Chapter Two

"I just know it, Chels," Raven griped later that day as she and Chelsea walked into the Baxters' kitchen. "My vision is going to come true." She opened the refrigerator door and grabbed two juice boxes from inside.

"Rae, would you stop panicking, please?" Chelsea said. "Just because Lawler asked her to sub doesn't mean she's going to do it. So let's talk about something else." Chelsea thought for a moment, tossing her shoulder-length red hair. "Is she an easy grader?" she asked.

Raven sighed in frustration as she headed into the living room. "It would just be too weird," she told Chelsea. "I know there has got to be a way to change this thing."

Just then, she spotted Cory sitting on the couch, watching TV.

An idea started to form in her mind. Raven glanced at Chelsea, who gave her an "oh yeah" smile. Plan Convince Mom Not To Teach was on.

"Hey, brother, how you doing?" Raven asked, sitting down on the couch beside Cory.

Cory looked at her warily.

"I'm going to need you to do me a favor," Raven went on in a voice like butter. "When Mom comes downstairs, I'm going to cough, and I want you to say, 'Mommy, please don't leave me all alone.'" Raven batted her eyelashes convincingly.

"Not a problem," Cory replied. "I do this for you and I get . . . ?" He looked hopefully at his crush-girl, Chelsea.

"Forget it," Chelsea snapped.

"Oooh, I like 'em feisty," Cory said, waggling his eyebrows.

"Two bucks or nothing," Raven said, snapping her gum.

"Deal," said Cory.

"Okay, here you go." Raven pulled the money from the pocket of her purple velvet flares and handed it over.

Cory cast a smooth glance at Chelsea and said, "This ain't over yet, baby."

Just then, Raven's mother came down the stairs. "Oh, Raven," she said, "that's just you popping your gum. I thought they were ripping up the sidewalk."

Raven stopped chewing.

"Listen, honey," Mrs. Baxter went on, "I thought about Mr. Lawler's offer, and if you have a problem with me subbing for a couple of days—"

"Oh, no, no, Mom," Raven said quickly.

"I'm totally fine with it. But I am a little concerned about my little brother. See, he gets home at 2:45, and if you sub, you wouldn't get home until almost 3:00. You know, when I was his age, you were there for me. And those fifteen minutes meant so much." Raven pretended to hold back tears. She took a shaky breath. "Thank you, Mom."

Dang, I think I need a box of tissues, Raven thought. This performance is so good, I'm even making myself cry. She gestured toward her little brother. "Let's just see how Cory feels," Raven said. She gave Cory the signal cough.

Nothing happened.

Raven coughed again.

"Wait," Cory said slowly, standing up from the couch. "Are you saying that for fifteen minutes, I'd be home all by myself?"

Raven glared at him, coughed again, and pointed to her mother.

But Cory wasn't paying attention. Suddenly, he had a vision of himself swinging into the living room on a jungle vine, then dropping into an armchair, where two gorgeous women fanned him with palm leaves. One of them held up a coconut drink for Cory to sip, while the other fed him a piece of pizza. . . .

Raven was coughing like crazy . . . and holding up a signal *fist* to remind Cory what would happen to him if he didn't go along with the plan.

"Oh, yeah," Cory said, lost in his daydream. "Don't worry about me, Mom. I'll be fine." He turned to Raven, who was hacking her head off. "I would do something about that cough," he told her before running up the stairs.

Raven stared after him. Ooh, little brother, she thought, you'd better watch out. Those fifteen minutes alone might not be as much fun as you think.

Chapter Three

"**I** don't want to go!" Raven wailed as Chelsea and Eddie dragged her into English class. She dug the heels of her boots into the linoleum. "I don't want to go!"

"Be brave," Eddie said, "your mom isn't even here yet. Just relax."

"Right, relax, relax," Raven whispered to herself, shaking the tension out of her shoulders. "She's not here. But she's in the building." Giving an involuntary shudder, Raven glanced around nervously. "I can feel her. She's getting closer . . ." Her voice rose hysterically. ". . . and closer and closer!" Raven clamped her hands over her eyes. "I can't see!"

"Rae!" Chelsea snapped, smacking Raven's hand away from her face.

Raven stared at the classroom around her. "It's a miracle!" she whispered.

Eddie rolled his eyes and sat down. He, at least, was looking forward to having Mrs. Baxter as their teacher. For the first time, the front row was safe. There wouldn't be any waterworks today.

Lucky my sight returned when it did, Raven thought as her favorite hottie walked by. "Heyyyy, Eric," she said with a grin.

Eric smiled. "Hey."

Raven shook her head as Eric walked off. "He is so . . ." She gritted her teeth, forcing out the word. "*Fine*."

Just then, Raven's mom walked into the room carrying an armload of books.

"Hello, class," she said brightly. Raven noticed that her mother wasn't wearing her usual relaxed clothing. Mrs. Baxter had traded in her casual jeans and T-shirt for a mustard-colored turtleneck and a plaid skirt. Very English-teachery, Raven thought with approval. Just please, Mama, don't do anything to embarrass me.

"I'm your substitute, Mrs. Baxter," Raven's mom went on, plunking the books on the desk.

A murmur of surprise went around the room.

"Today we're going to be working on *Romeo and Juliet*. Can anyone tell me what this play is about?" Mrs. Baxter asked, scanning the class. "Anyone?"

The students sank down in their seats.

If I go any lower, I'll be able to see the gum stuck to the bottom of my desk, Raven thought. She put a hand to the side of her face, hoping that it would somehow make her invisible.

No such luck. Mrs. Baxter looked right at Raven and said in a singsong voice, "I know someone who can. Raven?"

Reluctantly, Raven hauled herself to her feet. "Boy likes girl. Girl likes boy. They both die. Cry, cry, cry," she said quickly. "The end." She dove back into her seat, slouching as far down as she could.

"Good." Mrs. Baxter smiled nervously. "Fast. But good, honey."

Oh, no, she didn't, Raven thought, wincing at the word.

"I mean, *Raven*." Mrs. Baxter gave a little laugh and started to explain. "Well I called her 'honey' because she's my—"

Making it worse, Mom! Raven thought frantically. Making it worse!

Mrs. Baxter seemed to tune in to Raven's thought waves, because she waved her hands dismissively and said, "Oh, you know the story."

Yeah, the story of my miserable life, Raven thought, shaking her head. "Just one more day," she whispered to herself. "One more day."

"Romeo, Romeo," Mrs. Baxter read aloud in class the next morning, "wherefore art thou, Romeo?"

Raven chewed her gum frantically. Her mom was reading the balcony scene from *Romeo and Juliet*, and Raven had never been more embarrassed. It wasn't that Mrs. Baxter was bad—actually, she was reading with a lot of feeling. The words came alive in a way that they never had for Raven when she was just reading them on the page. That was the problem. Raven just wished her mother would try to be a bit more . . . *inconspicuous.*

"Deny thy father and refuse thy name,"

Mrs. Baxter went on, walking between the students' desks.

Max leaned over. "Raven," he whispered, "I know you're bummed out that your mom's here and all, but if it makes you feel any better . . ." He looked at Mrs. Baxter, his blue eyes wide in admiration. "She's a babe."

Okay, that does not make me feel better, Raven thought. That makes me feel like my breakfast is about to make a return appearance.

"That which we call a rose by any other name would smell as sweet," Mrs. Baxter read as she walked back to the front of the class.

"Sweeeet," Max murmured, sinking in his chair.

Looking up from her reading, Mrs. Baxter noticed the blank looks on her students' faces. "Okay," she said, "let me try and make this a little easier. If Shakespeare were writing today,

it might sound more like this. . . . Yo, Romeo!"
Mrs. Baxter shrieked in a high-pitched
Brooklyn accent.

Let me die, Raven thought as she tried to
hide behind her book. But her mother didn't
stop.

"Wassup?" Mrs. Baxter went on. "Where
you at? You better tell your daddy if he don't
like us together, then that's just too bad, 'cause
this Juliet ain't waitin' around for some fool in
tights named Romeo! You know what I'm
sayin'?"

The class cracked up.

Very funny, Raven thought, rolling her
eyes. I can't believe I'm sitting here listening to
my mother do her Rosie Perez imitation in my
English class. Could my life get any more
bizarre?

"And Romeo might sound like this," Mrs.
Baxter went on. "Do you believe the words

that are coming out of her mouth?" she said, sounding like Chris Tucker.

Yes, it did just get more bizarre, Raven thought. Make it stop! Make it stop! And all of you—she thought, glaring at her classmates, who were laughing their heads off—don't you see that you're only encouraging her? Stop it!

"Should I speak up and make a fool of myself?" Mrs. Baxter went on, translating the Shakespeare. "Or just let her go on and on about how fine she thinks I am?"

This is so unbelievably annoying, Raven thought, chomping her gum as though she were out for revenge.

"Raven," Mrs. Baxter said, sticking out her palm, "gum."

Raven spat her gum into her mother's hand.

"Three more hours," Raven said through gritted teeth. "Just three more hours."

Chapter Four

Finally, finally, finally, the last bell rang.

"I'm free!" Raven shouted, skipping into the hall. She grinned at Chelsea and Eddie, then slipped into a little victory groove. "No Mom. No more Mom!" she chanted, dancing with joy. "No more Mom! No more Mom! Hey—Mom!" she cried suddenly as Mrs. Baxter walked up behind her, joining Raven in her victory dance. Hope she didn't hear that, Raven thought as she straightened the purple fake fur trim on her jacket.

Mrs. Baxter smiled. "Hey."

"Hey, you know what?" Raven said. "These last two days, man. It's like, blink." Raven blinked dramatically. "Where'd they go?"

"I mean, I didn't see 'em," Chelsea agreed. "Did you see 'em?"

"I didn't see 'em. Did you?" Raven pointed at her mom.

Mrs. Baxter's smile widened. "Then I've got good news. I just spoke with Mr. Lawler and he offered me a permanent position." She put a Lawler-y emphasis on the Ps.

Raven actually felt the smile drop off her face, fall to the floor, and shatter into a million pieces. *Permanent position*, her mind echoed. Permanent, as in every day *for the rest of the year*.

Mrs. Baxter looked at Raven. "You okay with this?" she asked.

Raven cleared her throat as she chewed nervously on her gum. Okay, this is it, she thought. I just can't lie anymore. I can't deal with having my mom here all the time—I'll go nuts. But I have to be careful. I don't want to hurt her feelings.

Raven took her mother's hand and drew her aside. "Well," she admitted, "actually—"

Just then, Raven's skin began to prickle and the world seemed to freeze. . . .

Through her eye
The vision runs
Flash of future
Here it comes—

I'm in the kitchen at home. I'm sitting with Mom. I guess we've been talking.

She sure looks happy. Yo, Mom, what are you grinning about?

"Raven," Mom says, taking my hand, "I love this job."

Oh, snap!

Raven found herself back in the present, facing a dilemma. She could still tell her mother the truth. But she loves teaching, Raven thought. She would be so disappointed. I just can't do that to her.

Mrs. Baxter was looking at Raven, smiling expectantly.

Raven made her choice. "I couldn't be happier," she lied.

"Thanks, sweetie." Mrs. Baxter put her arms around Raven and hugged her tight.

Raven chomped on her gum. It was turning into a nervous habit—and she had a lot to be nervous about these days.

Mrs. Baxter pulled away. "Honey, gum," she said.

Reflexively, Chelsea stuck out her hand, and Raven spat her gum into it.

"Well, I'm going home to tell your little brother," Mrs. Baxter said brightly. "I just hope he understands."

Raven rolled her eyes. She was pretty sure

that at that moment Cory was enjoying his fifteen minutes home alone dancing around the Baxters' living room in a conga line of ten-year-olds.

Well, Raven thought, at least somebody's happy.

Chapter Five

"**I** don't get it, Rae," Chelsea said Monday morning as she and Raven walked down the hall. "Your mom asked if you had a problem with her teaching here. Why didn't you just tell her how you felt?"

"Chelsea, you did not see my vision." Raven sighed. "First of all, she loves this job. And everybody in class loves her, too. I just can't take that from her."

"You're a good daughter, Rae," Chelsea said.

"Thanks," Raven said. She thought for a moment. "Maybe we can get her fired," she added.

Chelsea scowled.

"I was just kidding!" Raven protested. "Can't I dream?"

Chelsea headed off to her next class, and Raven started toward her locker.

Just then, Max jogged up behind her and tapped her on the shoulder. "Raven, I've been thinking," he said. He took a deep breath. "I don't mind that your mom has kids." Max nodded thoughtfully, digging his hands into his pockets. "I'm good with kids."

Raven glared at him. "Max, my mama is married, okay?" she snapped. "Let it go before it gets ugly." As she looked him up and down, Raven felt a familiar dizzy feeling. A second later, she shoved a folder at him. "And you're gonna need this."

Max frowned at the folder, confused, but took it anyway. Suddenly, his eyes lit up. "Oooh," he said, catching sight of something shiny on the floor. "Lucky penny!"

As he bent over to pick it up, the seat of his jeans ripped in two, just as Raven had predicted.

Max looked around, embarrassed. Then, holding the folder Raven had given him over his rear, he scuttled off down the hall.

Guess that penny wasn't so lucky after all, Raven thought as she watched him go. Just then, she saw something that made her *own* eyes light up. "Heyyy, Eric," she said.

Eric leaned against the lockers next to Raven's. "Hey."

Raven sighed dreamily. "Hi."

Eric smiled. "I was wondering if, after school, you know, you'd like to—"

"Eric," Mrs. Baxter said, walking past, "nice report."

He smiled proudly at Raven.

"But next time," Mrs. Baxter went on, "maybe you could hand it in without the pizza stains."

What was that about getting my mama fired? Raven thought furiously. She stared at her mother in disbelief.

Eric shook his head. "I don't know what's up with that new teacher," he complained once Mrs. Baxter had walked away.

Raven scoffed. "Tell me about it."

"Oh, and honey," Mrs. Baxter said, circling back to face Raven, "I'm going to be home a little late. You mind starting dinner? I've got chicken in the—"

"Got it, got it, got it!" Raven said through clenched teeth.

Nodding, Mrs. Baxter walked off.

"I don't know what that woman was talking about," Raven told Eric once her mother was out of earshot. She batted her eyelashes, and prompted, "You were saying?"

Eric looked uncomfortable. "I gotta go," he said. "Later."

"I had him!" Raven wailed, slouching against her locker. "Man, I had him. He was in my grasp. I had him."

She slammed through the double doors on the way to class, muttering, "Mommified."

Later that morning, Raven sat in English class, scribbling furiously. She just had to let her friends know what had happened with Eric. It was horrible! *Having my mom here is totally bustin' my game*, Raven wrote. *I hate it!*

"Okay, before we get started," Mrs. Baxter announced, "I just wanted to let you know that I'm going to be your teacher for the rest of the year."

The class burst into cheers and whoops.

Everyone except for Raven, that is. She was still writing madly.

"Is all of that for me?" Mrs. Baxter said,

busting out her Rosie Perez voice. "That's for me? Aw, you stop it. You stop it!"

The class quieted down.

"What happen?" Mrs. Baxter demanded, still using her Brooklyn accent. "Why you stop?"

I just don't want her here, Raven wrote. She pressed so hard, her ballpoint nearly ripped through the paper. *She's not funny, she's embarrassing, she's . . . I hate this!!!!!*

Raven finished off with a series of underlines and exclamation marks, then passed the note to Eddie.

Eddie unfolded the note and quickly read it. "Man, Rae," Eddie whispered. "This is cold."

"Pass it to Chelsea," Raven commanded.

Eddie waited until Mrs. Baxter wasn't looking, then tapped Chelsea on the shoulder. She unfolded the note and scanned the first line. "Wow," Chelsea said, looking over at Raven.

"Okay, guys," Mrs. Baxter announced. "If you will take out your vocabulary list and review it, I will collect the homework. Thank you."

Chelsea hid the note beneath her report as Mrs. Baxter started collecting the homework at the far end of the room.

The rest of Chelsea's row passed their homework forward, and Chelsea dropped their assignments on top of her own. A moment later, Mrs. Baxter grabbed the stack of homework from Chelsea's desk . . . and Raven's note with it!

Raven and Chelsea exchanged horrified looks.

Oh, man! Raven thought. If my mom reads what I wrote . . . Don't think about it, she told herself. I will just not let it happen. I have to get it back. I have to. She buried her face in her hands. Just think of something. . . .

Fifty minutes later, the bell rang, and Raven, Chelsea, and Eddie trooped out the door, hardly able to tear their eyes away from the stack of homework on Mrs. Baxter's desk.

A moment later, they trooped right back in, grinning. Raven had a plan.

"Mrs. Baxter, may I just say how much I enjoyed doing that homework assignment?" Eddie said, smiling sweetly.

Mrs. Baxter smiled.

"But I'd like to change one little bitty thing," Eddie went on. "Can I see Chelsea's homework?"

Mrs. Baxter's smile tightened. "That would be called cheating," she said.

Chelsea laughed. "That's not what he meant," she said quickly.

Mrs. Baxter eyed her coolly as she picked up the stack of homework. "What did he mean?"

Chelsea blinked. "I don't know."

Time to come up with an escape strategy, Raven thought. "Gotcha!" Raven said quickly. She reached out and grabbed the homework that was in her mother's hands. Her mother yanked it back, but Raven didn't let go.

"That was all a joke," Raven said as she yanked on the homework again. "It's just a trick we play on all the subs. But you didn't fall for it."

Raven's mother yanked back. The woman is stronger than she looks, Raven thought as she gave a final yank—and the note came free.

Here it is! Raven thought triumphantly, looking at the note in her hand. "There it goes," she groaned as her mother snatched the piece of paper from Raven.

"Thank you," Mrs. Baxter said, sticking the paper back into the pile of homework. "And you can all have your papers back after I grade them in the morning."

"As it should be, Mrs. Baxter," Chelsea said, giving Mrs. Baxter a "way to go" look.

"Spoken like a true teacher," Eddie put in, laughing heartily.

"I'm proud of you, Mom," Raven added as the three friends hustled toward the classroom door.

What's she doing with it? Raven thought, still eyeing the note from the doorway. Her mother caught her looking, so Raven smiled and gave her a little wave. She pretended to leave, but paused at the doorway, watching as her mother stuck the pile of homework in her desk drawer. And there it goes, Raven thought. Upper right-hand side.

"Operation Note Rescue," Raven announced once she had joined her friends out in the hallway. "We attack at dawn."

Chapter Six

"**R**eady?" Raven asked in her best army commander voice early the next morning.

Raven, Eddie, and Chelsea were standing in the hallway outside their English classroom. Chelsea had even worn purple camouflage pants in honor of their mission.

"Ready," Eddie and Chelsea chorused.

"We're going in," Raven declared. She turned to the classroom door and tried the knob. "No we're not. It's locked."

"It's locked," Chelsea announced in her own army commander voice.

"I just said that," Raven barked.

"I know," Chelsea barked back. For some

reason, neither one of them could stop using that voice.

There has to be a way in, Raven thought, turning back to the door. And then she saw it—the transom above the door was open. Raven was pretty sure she could shimmy through it. "Give me a boost," Raven said.

Chelsea and Eddie laced their fingers together to make a step for Raven, and together they lifted her toward the transom. Raven hauled herself halfway through. Hanging by her waist, she reached down toward the doorknob. "Get it!" She grunted. "Get it!"

Chelsea and Eddie watched nervously. Raven was almost there. . . .

"Good morning," said a voice behind them.

Eddie and Chelsea spun around. "Uh, hi, Mr. Lawler," Chelsea said, loud enough for Raven to hear.

Oh, man! Raven thought. Hanging upside

down, she looked back through the glass in the door and saw Eddie and Chelsea talking to the principal. She stifled a grunt as the edge of the transom dug into her stomach. Don't look up, she begged the principal silently.

"We're doing nothing wrong, sir," Eddie announced.

"Well, I'm pleased to see my pupils here so early." Principal Lawler rocked back on his heels and let the saliva fly. "As principal, I arrive promptly at six-thirty and do a thorough inspection of the premises with my master key. Watch." He pulled a key from a chain on his waist. Putting the key in the lock, he swung open the classroom door. "Open!"

As the door opened into the room, Raven tipped back so he wouldn't see her draped through the transom above. Her legs dangled behind Lawler's back.

"Close!" Lawler said, closing the door.

Raven tipped forward, lifting her legs up just as Lawler turned.

"Open!" Lawler swung open the door again and poked his head into the room.

Please tell me that this is good for the abs, Raven thought as she tipped backward again. Because I am getting some kind of workout here.

"Looks good in here," Lawler said, pulling the door shut. "Close. Well, better finish patrolling the place. Toodles." Giving them a little wave, he walked off down the hall.

"Hey, Rae," Eddie called up to Raven, who was looking at them upside down through the glass in the door. "While you're hanging there, could you open the door?"

What does he think I'm doing here? Raven thought. But she decided to let it go.

"No problem," she told him. She grunted and leaned toward the knob. This time, she managed to reach it.

Instantly, Chelsea and Eddie burst into the classroom and hurried over to the teacher's desk. Chelsea yanked at the drawer that held their homework assignments. "It's locked," she announced.

"Where's the key?" Eddie asked.

Um, hello? Raven thought from her perch over the door. "Guys?" she called.

"I don't have the key," Chelsea told Eddie.

"What are we gonna do?" Eddie asked.

"Guys!" Raven shouted. She tried to pull herself up, but it was no good—she was stuck. She couldn't back out, and there was no way she was going to let herself fall face-first onto the linoleum.

"Well, try to pry it open," Chelsea suggested, paying no attention to Raven.

Eddie used a letter opener, but the drawer wouldn't budge. "No good. What are we gonna do?"

"Guys!" Raven hollered. "Hanging like a bat over here."

Finally noticing that their friend was still upside down over the door, Eddie and Chelsea hurried over to help her. They managed to pull her down safely.

Moments later, the three friends found themselves hauling the heavy wooden desk down the hallway.

"So, what's the plan?" Eddie asked when they stopped to rest. Raven always had a plan.

"To get this desk as far away from my mom as possible," Raven announced. True, as a plan, it needed work. But it was all she had.

"But, Rae," Chelsea pointed out, "this is school property."

"I know," Raven snapped. "That's why we'll be moving it *very carefully.*" They headed down the hall. "Door, door, door!" Raven called as Eddie backed into a couple of swinging doors.

Raven and her friends hauled the desk up some stairs.

They hauled it into a corner, smashing Raven and Chelsea against a wall.

They hauled it through the auditorium.

They hauled it down some stairs.

And they ended up in the same hallway where they had started.

"I don't mean to bug y'all or anything," Eddie griped as *he* got smashed against a wall, "but can we come up with a better plan?"

But no one had a better plan. So they kept hauling the desk around. "Right!" Raven shouted, steering them around a corner. "No, right!"

The friends hauled the desk past a janitor, who was transporting some garbage cans on a dolly. Suddenly, they stopped. *A dolly.*

They waited for the janitor to walk away, then put the desk on the dolly and started to push it toward the exit.

"Hey!" the janitor called, catching sight of them. Quickly, they let go of the dolly, which kept on rolling.

Thinking fast, Raven took a running leap onto the desk. It started rolling faster.

"This can't be good!" Raven wailed as the dolly slammed through the exit doors.

Chelsea and Eddie tore after her.

The dolly, the desk, and Raven bounced down a flight of stairs and out into the school-yard. Screaming her head off, Raven rolled past the bike rack and out into the parking lot, where she smashed into a parked truck. Luckily, neither Raven nor the desk was hurt. Much.

As they hauled the desk back into the school, they ran into Principal Lawler for the second time that morning.

"Where did that desk come from?" Lawler asked.

The three friends stared down at the desk.

I give up, Raven thought dimly. I am too tired to think up an explanation for this.

"Actually, Mr. Lawler," Chelsea said, stepping up to the plate, "this desk came from a tree, until mankind cut it down with no regard to nature and all its wonder—"

Okay, I un-give up, Raven thought. Clearly I am needed here. "What she's trying to say, Mr. Lawler," Raven broke in, "is that we found it in the parking lot and we're just, you know, bringing it back."

"Well, pick me up and put me down!" Lawler sprayed. "This is my old desk. Solid, sturdy . . . except for this pesky drawer." He gave the drawer with the homework in it a bang, and it shot open.

A heavenly choir chorused in Raven's mind.

There was the stack of homework with the note hidden inside, practically in her grasp. All she had to do was come up with a diversion. . . .

The principal was about to slam the drawer closed, when Raven pointed behind him and shouted, "Wait! Stop!"

Lawler turned to look behind him. Raven dug in the drawer and pulled out the note. Crumpling it up, she hid it behind her back.

"Who were you talking to?" Mr. Lawler asked, turning back to Raven.

"Uh . . . she was just singing that new cool song," Chelsea said quickly. "Yeah, how does that go?" She turned to her friends, gesturing for them to help her out. "You know, um . . ."

Getting it, Eddie started to beatbox.

"Wait! Stop!" Chelsea shouted, dancing to the beat.

"Where you going?" Raven sang.

"Stop! Wait!" Chelsea went on.

"I'm a comin'," Raven sang. "Yeah."

"Yeah!" Chelsea and Raven said together.

Eddie added the topper. "Boy-ee."

"I like that!" Lawler said brightly. He slammed the desk drawer shut. "Come on, Mr. Thomas, let's bring this baby back upstairs. Show me how you do that . . ." As he and Eddie began to push the dolly, Lawler busted into his own version of beatboxing, which was pretty heavy on the spray.

Interesting effect, Raven thought as she watched the principal cover Eddie in spittle. But I don't think it's the future of hip-hop.

Chapter Seven

As Chelsea and Raven walked down the hall, Chelsea read the note aloud. "'And every single second my mom's here, my life gets worse and worse. If I see her face in my class one more time, I'm going to . . . scream.'" Finishing the note, Chelsea looked up at Raven sympathetically.

"Now you know why I don't want her to read the note," Raven said sadly.

"Rae, I know it's really hard having her here," Chelsea said, struggling to find something supportive to say. "But . . . I don't know. Maybe it'll get better."

Raven shrugged. "Maybe. But maybe it won't. Look, I love my mom, and I love hanging out with her. Just not here. Here, I'm Raven, but when she's here, I'm . . . Mrs. Baxter's daughter."

"Rae," Chelsea said gently, "your mom is, like, so cool. She'll understand."

"I know," Raven admitted. "But she's so happy here. I guess I'll just have to get used to it, huh?"

Nodding, Chelsea hooked her arm through Raven's and the two started off down the hall.

It sure is a relief to have that note back, Raven thought. I'm so glad Mom didn't read it.

But what Raven didn't know was that Mrs. Baxter had been right behind them when Chelsea read the note aloud. And she had heard every word.

After school that day, Mrs. Baxter found Raven sitting in the kitchen, flipping through her history book.

"Hey, honey . . . you got a minute?" she said.

Raven looked up. "Sure."

"You know," Mrs. Baxter said as she slid onto the stool next to Raven's, "being at school with you got me thinking about when I was your age. I used to get away with so much stuff. I had this one teacher, Mr. Swenson, and I did the best imitation of him. 'Enunciate, Ms. Baxter,'" she mimicked in a nasal voice. "'Enunciate.' I mean, I had the whole class cracking up."

Raven gave her mother a doubtful look. "You?"

"Your mama had a life!" Mrs. Baxter replied. "And if there were cute boys in the hall, I'd be talking to them. Like you . . . with your friend, Eric." She gave her daughter a sympathetic smile. "I kind of blew that for you, didn't I?"

Raven tried to play it cool. "You know," she

said, shrugging. But the truth came out anyway. "Yeah, you did, Mama, you did."

"Honey, I had a great time when I was in school," Mrs. Baxter said. "But it would have been really weird if my mom were around."

Raven looked down at the counter. She didn't want to hurt her mother's feelings, but she couldn't exactly disagree.

"That's why I'm not going to take this teaching job," Mrs. Baxter finished.

"What?" Raven looked up, startled. Oh, no, she thought. I blew it! Mom's going to give up the job she loves, and it's all my fault. "Mama, all the kids think you're great."

"Raven," Mrs. Baxter said, squeezing her daughter's hand, "I love this job."

"I know," Raven said. "Being a teacher." That's why I feel so bad, Mama. Way to rub it in!

"No," Mrs. Baxter said. "Being your mom."

Oh, Raven thought, suddenly understanding her vision. I had it wrong all along! She really does understand. Reaching out, Raven gave her mother a huge hug.

"And when I do go back to teaching," Mrs. Baxter continued, "I'll make sure it's at a different school. Promise."

She put out her fist and, to Raven's surprise, did the elaborate handshake that Raven usually reserved for her best friends.

"Bam!" Mrs. Baxter and Raven cried together.

"Go on, Mama," Raven said with a grin, "that's tight." Dang, when did my mom learn that handshake? Raven wondered. She must have been watching me even closer than I realized.

Mrs. Baxter slapped her chest, then flicked her hand as she hopped off the stool. "What, you think you the only one that could get some dap?" she asked in her most outrageous

Rosie Perez imitation, snapping her fingers.

"Hey, what was that last thing you did?" Raven asked. "You know, with the—" Raven tried doing the hand-flick thing.

"Girl," Mrs. Baxter quipped in Brooklynese as she left the room, "if you think you're gonna jack my moves, think again."

"Mom!" Raven cried. "Mama, wait!"

Hey, Raven thought, chasing after her mother, maybe there are a few things I wouldn't mind learning from my mama, after all.

Gaze into the future and take a sneak peek at the next *That's So Raven* story. . . .

Adapted by Alice Alfonsi
Based on the series created by
Michael Poryes
Susan Sherman
Based on the teleplay written
by Dava Savel & Carla Banks Waddles

"Come on, *reach*," Raven Baxter urged her best friend, Chelsea Daniels. "You're so close."

"Rae, I can't do it!" wailed Chelsea.

Girl, thought Raven, don't give up on me now!

Strapped into safety harnesses, the two friends clung to a tall rock wall in the Bayside school gym. The top of the wall was only inches away.

"You can do it. Yes, you can," Raven coaxed Chelsea, who was struggling just below her. "A little bit further."

Chelsea knew Raven was counting on her. Straining, she reached up with all her strength—to hold the tube of lip gloss just a little bit higher.

"Got it!" Raven cried, pulling the applicator wand free. "Oooh, girl, Mocha Frost, my favorite." She brushed the shimmering gloss across her lips, then glanced at her classmates on the gym floor below. "Now I can look *good* coming down," she whispered to Chelsea. "See you at the bottom!"

As their entire class looked on, Raven and Chelsea made their final pull to the top of the rock wall, then rappelled down like action heroines.

When the girls reached the floor, their teacher praised their performance. No sweat, Raven thought confidently. Well, maybe a *little* sweat, she added, dabbing at her forehead. Thanks to Chels, however, her lips were looking totally fresh.

Exchanging a high five, Chelsea and Raven strutted out of the gym to hit the showers. They slammed through the swinging doors, then suddenly stopped. Dead ahead lay a treacherous path.

"Maybe we should take the long way to the locker room," whispered Chelsea, "and avoid, you know . . ."

"The Jock Block," Raven finished for her.

"Uh-huh," said Chelsea, nervously chewing her bottom lip.

The Jock Block, also known as the Highway

of Hotties, was a short strip of hallway lined with lockers that belonged to the members of Bayside's basketball, football, and baseball teams.

Raven looked over at the twenty or so good-looking Bayside Barracudas who were talking and laughing in the corridor. She had to agree with Chelsea. "There is no way that I'm walking through *all that* looking like *all this*," Raven whispered, tugging at her loose gym clothes. Her uniform was damp with perspiration, ridiculously oversized, and an embarrassingly bright shade of yellow.

"I know," replied Chelsea. "I mean, my hair's all a mess, I'm, like, really sweaty, and, FYI, you kind of smell a little . . . well, actually, you smell *a lot.*"

Raven frowned, raised her arm, and sniffed. Okay, so her dandelion yellow sweatshirt didn't smell as fresh as a daisy, she thought, but it wasn't *that* bad. With hands on her hips, she glared at Chelsea.

"Just keepin' it real, Rae," Chelsea said, crossing her arms in the lamest hip-hop pose Raven had ever seen. "Keepin' it real."

Dang, thought Raven, I hook up my country friend with some homey lingo, and *this* is my payback. "Hey, Chelsea," she snapped, "I taught you that phrase. Don't use it against me."

Just then, the girls noticed their best friend, Eddie Thomas, coming toward them—well, actually, *hobbling* toward them—from the other end of the Jock Block. He was wearing green cargo pants, a long sweater, and a white bandage on his right foot. He struggled with a pair of crutches as he made his way down the hall.

"Look, Eddie hurt his foot," said Chelsea.

"*And* it's rock-climbing week in gym," Raven pointed out.

"Think there's a connection?" asked Chelsea.

Raven arched one eyebrow. Eddie had never been very fond of heights. Whenever they went to the mall, he refused to go *near* the glass elevators. And during last year's rock-climbing week at Bayside, Eddie had been absent every day. He claimed he'd had to attend his Uncle Fredo's funeral in Kansas City—but Raven was pretty sure Eddie didn't *have* an Uncle Fredo.

The girls eyed Eddie's bandaged foot and crutches suspiciously. "Hmmm," they both said, putting their fingers to their chins.

"Watch this," Raven whispered to Chelsea. Cupping her hands around her freshly Mocha Frosted lips, she shouted, "Hey, Eddie! There's free pizza in the cafeteria!"

"Free pizza!" Eddie cried.

He picked up his crutches and began to

hurry down the hall. As soon as he saw Raven laughing, however, he realized he'd been played. He slid to a stop and slowly lifted his bandaged foot—the one he'd just been running on.

"Um, what I meant to say was . . . *Ow*," he told them, as he put the crutches back under his arms.

Shaking her head, Raven replied, "Eddie, it's a wall. Climb it."

"Hey, I don't do heights, okay?" Eddie informed her. "Birds gotta fly, fish gotta swim, and Eddie's gotta stay on the ground."

"Come on, Eddie," Chelsea said brightly, "you're good in every other sport. Basketball, baseball . . ."

"Again, all on *the ground*!" he pointed out.

Suddenly, Raven froze. As the world around her blurred, a scene from the future shimmered into focus. . . .

Through her eye
The vision runs
Flash of future
Here it comes—

I see the school gym. Hey, the rock wall is still up. Guess whatever I'm seeing is going to happen this week.

Now I see some guy climbing the wall. Wait—I cannot believe what I'm seeing! It's Eddie! He's almost there—now he's at the top. He reaches out and smacks the coach's "victory" button, beaming as the siren and red light go off.

All right, Eddie! You're the man!

My boy looks so happy. "I made it!" he shouts as he pumps his fist in victory.

When Raven came out of her vision, her face broke into a wide grin.

"Eddie, I just saw you climbing the wall," she told him. "You're going to make it all the way to the top!"

"Really?" asked Eddie.

Raven nodded.

"You know what this means?" asked Eddie.

Raven and Chelsea shook their heads.

Eddie dropped his crutches and raised his palms to the ceiling. "Glory! I'm healed! I can walk!" he declared with more theatrical flair than a revival tent preacher. He gave Raven a huge grin. "I *love* that my best friend is psychic!"

Twenty minutes later, Eddie was clinging to the rock wall in the gym. He'd only managed to climb a few feet up before stark terror had gripped him and he'd squeezed his eyes shut. Below him, every single guy in his class was doubled over with laughter.

"What's the matter, Eddie?" yelled one of the jocks. "Afraid of heights?"

Through tightly clenched teeth, Eddie muttered, "I *hate* that my best friend is psychic!"

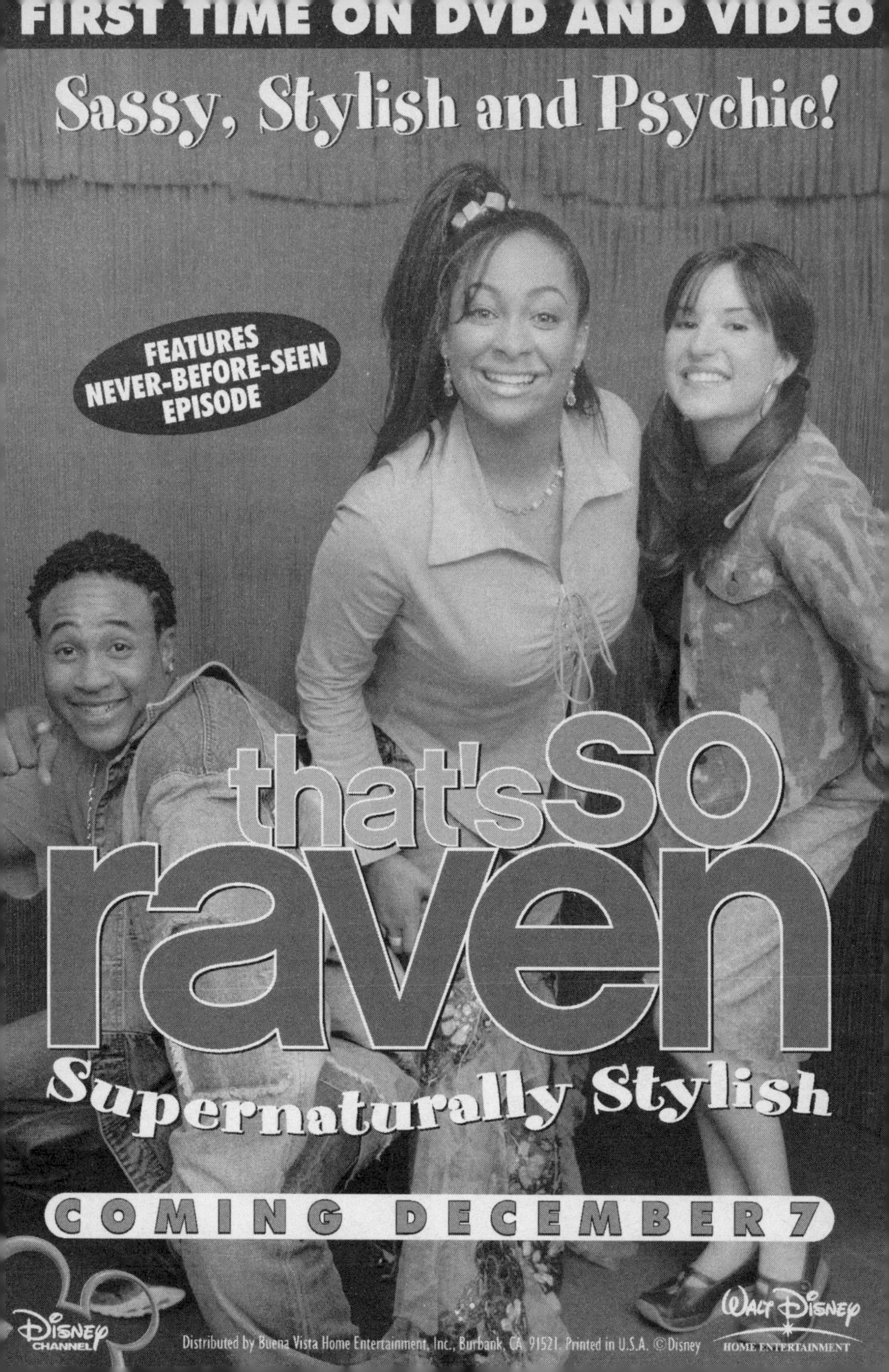

FIRST TIME ON DVD AND VIDEO
Sassy, Stylish and Psychic!
FEATURES NEVER-BEFORE-SEEN EPISODE
that's so raven
Supernaturally Stylish
COMING DECEMBER 7
DISNEY CHANNEL
Distributed by Buena Vista Home Entertainment, Inc., Burbank, CA 91521. Printed in U.S.A. ©Disney
WALT DISNEY HOME ENTERTAINMENT

Get Cheetah Power!

the Cheetah ★ Girls

Includes An Alternate Ending & Exclusive Behind-The-Scenes Look

Groove to the sound
of all your favorite shows

Disney Channel Soundtrack Series

Disney's
Kim Possible
TV Soundtrack

The Cheetah Girls
TV Soundtrack

Lizzie McGuire
TV Soundtrack

Pixel Perfect
Soundtrack

Also, look for...

- *The Proud Family* TV Series Soundtrack
- *That's So Raven* TV Series Soundtrack

Collect them all!

Wake up.
Go to school.
Save the world.

W.i.t.c.h
Will   Irma   Taranee   Cornelia   Hay Lin

The magic of friendship

The new book series · Make some powerful friends at www.clubwitch.com